Disney's classic *Cinderella* was first released in February 1950, the twelfth movie in the Walt Disney Animated Classics series. Based on a seventeenth-century fairy tale by Charles Perrault, the film was a huge commercial success that allowed Disney to finance a number of other movie and television productions. Among its many accolades, the film was nominated for three Academy Awards®—Best Sound, Original Music Score, and Best Song.

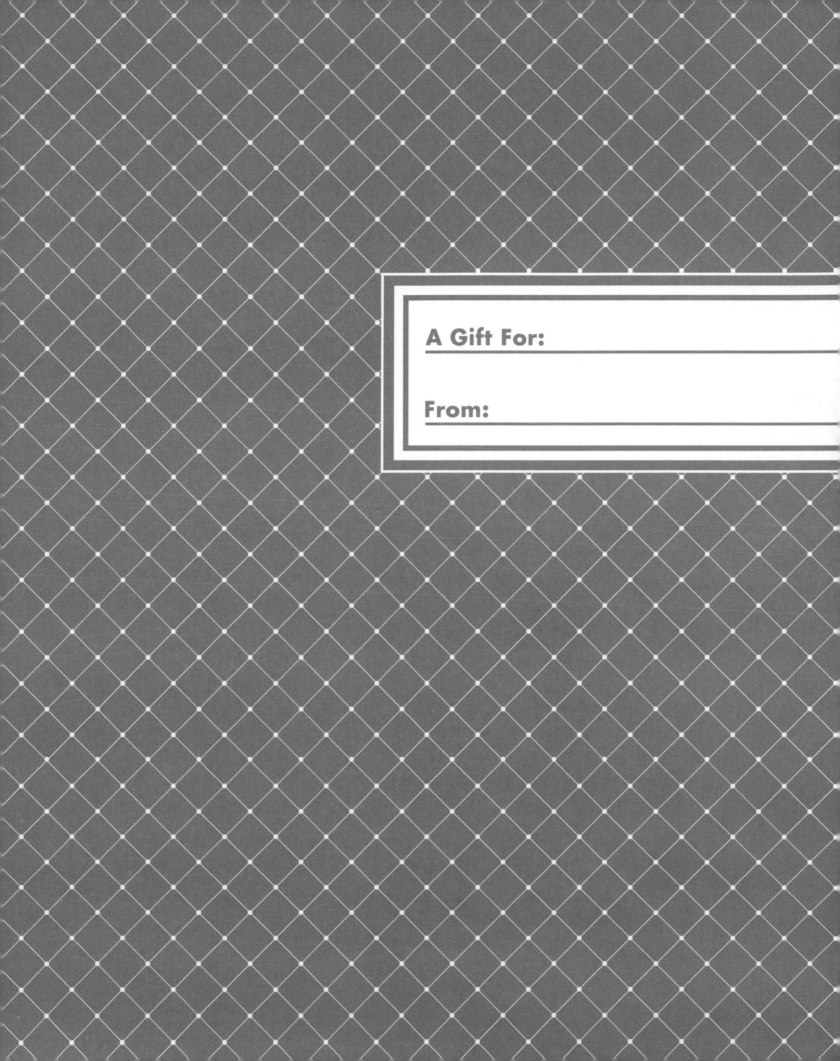

A Gift For:
_____

From:
_____

Published by Hallmark Gift Books,
a division of Hallmark Cards, Inc.,
Kansas City, MO 64141
Visit us on the Web at Hallmark.com.

Editorial Strategist: Delia Berrigan
Editor: Chelsea Fogleman
Art Director: Chris Opheim
Designer: Scott Swanson
Production Designer: Dan Horton

ISBN: 978-1-59530-532-9
BOK1223

Printed and bound in China
OCT12

Disney
Cinderella

Hallmark
gift books

Once upon a time, a beautiful girl named Cinderella lived in a faraway land with her devoted father, a widower. He remarried so Cinderella could have a stepmother and stepsisters.

But when her father died suddenly, a brokenhearted
Cinderella quickly discovered that her stepmother, Lady
Tremaine, was cold, cruel, and bitterly jealous of
Cinderella's charm and beauty.

As time went by, Cinderella became a servant in her own home. Yet, with each dawn she found new hope that someday her dreams of happiness would come true.

And despite how her stepfamily treated
her, Cinderella remained ever gentle and
kind. Her many devoted animal friends
helped her get dressed each day.

Not so far away, at the palace, there was a king who was upset that the royal prince still was unmarried. The King told the Grand Duke to invite every eligible maiden to a ball so his son could find a bride.

A palace messenger brought a royal invitation to Cinderella's house. Lady Tremaine grabbed the invitation from Cinderella and read, "By royal command, every eligible maiden is to attend."

"Why, that means I can go too!" exclaimed Cinderella.

Her stepsisters, Anastasia and Drizella, laughed, but Lady Tremaine agreed Cinderella could go—if she finished her chores and found something suitable to wear.

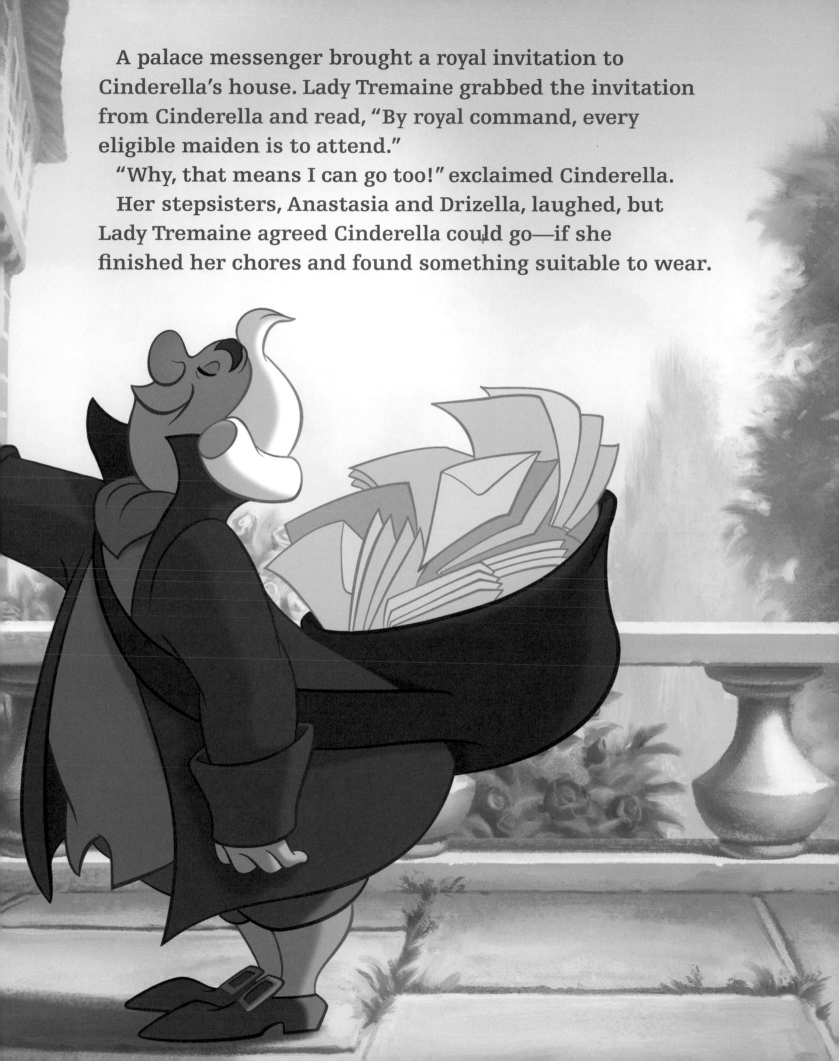

In the attic, Cinderella found a dress of her mother's. It was a bit old-fashioned, but Cinderella could fix it. She wouldn't have time now, though. Her stepmother was calling her again. The dress would have to wait.

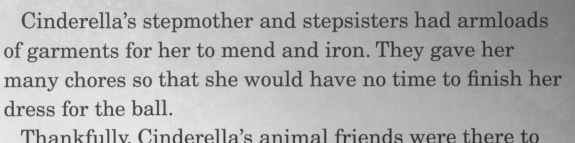

Cinderella's stepmother and stepsisters had armloads of garments for her to mend and iron. They gave her many chores so that she would have no time to finish her dress for the ball.

Thankfully, Cinderella's animal friends were there to help! They retrieved the stepsisters' discarded sash and beads. With just a little work, they turned Cinderella's simple dress into a fabulous ball gown!

Cinderella was so thrilled when she saw her
new dress. "Surprise!" her animal friends shouted.
   "Oh, thank you so much!" Cinderella cried
with delight.

But when Anastasia and Drizella saw Cinderella, they flew into a jealous rage. They ripped the dress, pulling off the sash and yanking the beads. Lady Tremaine just stood and watched.

Now Cinderella had no hope of going to the ball and meeting the Prince. She ran, heartbroken, to the garden and sobbed. "There's nothing left to believe in," she said. "Nothing!"

Suddenly a comforting presence appeared. She was
Cinderella's Fairy Godmother! And she was there because
Cinderella really hadn't given up believing.

Cinderella's Fairy Godmother insisted that Cinderella was going to the ball. She waved her magic wand and turned a simple pumpkin into an elegant coach, and the mice into horses!

The Fairy Godmother pointed her magic wand at Cinderella and said, "Bibbidi-bobbidi-boo!" Suddenly Cinderella was wearing a beautiful dress and sparkling glass slippers!

And then, Cinderella was off to the ball! The Fairy Godmother warned her to be home before midnight when everything would change back to normal.

At the palace, one young woman after another was called to step forward and meet the Prince. Anastasia and Drizella took their turn together. They curtsied before the Prince, but he was looking at someone behind them. He was looking at Cinderella.

Cinderella was the most beautiful girl the Prince had ever seen. He hurried to her side, and soon the two were dancing and dancing, gazing deeply into each other's eyes.

Then the Prince took Cinderella for a moonlit stroll across the bridge. The two were falling in love.

Cinderella had lost all track of time. It was nearly midnight!
"Good-bye!" she said to the Prince as she hurried away.
Both the Prince and the Grand Duke tried to stop her, but
Cinderella ran off, losing a glass slipper along the way.

Cinderella hurried into her waiting coach.
When the horses had galloped some distance
from the palace, the clock struck midnight!

Everyone and everything suddenly turned back to normal again. But Cinderella still had one glass slipper. She smiled and thanked the Fairy Godmother for a magical evening.

Back at the palace, the King was furious that the girl his son now loved had vanished without anyone knowing who she was. He demanded she be found.

The next morning, Lady Tremaine told her daughters that the Grand Duke was searching for the girl who lost the glass slipper. Whoever fit the slipper perfectly would marry the Prince!

Cinderella went to her room not quite believing what she had just heard. The Prince had fallen in love with her, just as she had fallen in love with him! Suddenly Lady Tremaine appeared. Without a word, she locked Cinderella in her room and pocketed the key. Lady Tremaine realized Cinderella was the girl the Prince was looking for!

Luckily, Cinderella's animal friends managed to get the key just as the Grand Duke arrived at the house.

The Grand Duke explained that every maiden in the kingdom must try on the glass slipper. The Duke's assistant helped Anastasia and Drizella as they each tried on the slipper. But they could not squeeze their big feet into the delicate little shoe.

Just as the Grand Duke was about to leave, Cinderella appeared at the top of the stairs. Her animal friends had freed her just in time!

Lady Tremaine tripped the footman and the glass slipper shattered before Cinderella could try it on. But that didn't matter. Cinderella still had the other slipper in her pocket. It was a perfect fit!

A royal wedding was quickly arranged.
Cinderella and the Prince were married
to the delight of the King and all
Cinderella's animal friends.

Cinderella's dreams had come true at last.
She and her prince lived happily ever after.

If you have enjoyed this book
or it has touched your life in some way,
we would love to hear from you.

Please send your comments to:
Hallmark Book Feedback
P.O. Box 419034
Mail Drop 215
Kansas City, MO 64141

Or e-mail us at:
booknotes@hallmark.com